DISCIPLES BOOK ONE:
NEW DAY

George Allen Blacken, Sr.

Apostolic Pentecostal Alliance Books LLC

WALDORF, MARYLAND

Printed in the United States of America

Published by Apostolic Pentecostal Alliance Books LLC, Maryland
www.apabooksllc.com

The Apostolic Pentecostal Alliance Books LLC name, logo, and colophon are the trademarks of Apostolic Pentecostal Alliance Books LLC.

ISBN: 978-0-9989630-4-4 (Printed Edition)
ISBN: 978-0-9989630-5-1 (E-Book Edition)

First Edition 2018

Write inquiries to:

Apostolic Pentecostal Alliance Books LLC
150 Post Office Road
P.O. Box 1813
Waldorf, MD 20601

Table of Contents

Chapter 1: Close Call

"They are going to get you this time!" you say to yourself. You usually don't worry, but why else would they be at the school in your classroom? God's Enforcers (G.E.s) brought the law to several of your peers screaming throughout the halls. You don't know who is a disciple these days.

"Stay calm class. Just do what G.E. tells you when they come in," Mr. Winsom instructed. He's right. Some of the screams were accompanied by thumping footsteps silenced by the firing of electro shocks and lasers. "No one will be harmed unless you are a disciple."

"Kids, don't try to be adults or martyrs today," said an approaching G.E. officer. The thumping of your heart suddenly exceeds the surrounding footsteps. "One of you needs to be rehabilitated. Take him away!"

"No! There must be a mistake!" Mr. Winsom blurted. "Mr. Winsom!" the class shouted as two G.E. officers dragged him away. "Shut up and stay in your seats!" The shouting G.E. officer walks down your row. "Mr. Winsom has been harboring disciples for years," the G.E. officer said. He puts his hand on your shoulder. "Jerry Redmon come with us." Everyone is surprised to hear your real name.

You slam the textbook on your desk shut and it clicks. The light blinds everyone but you. You were trained for this. Mr. Winsom left the window open. That is how G.E. knew he was one of us.

After the light fades, you are already out of the window and running on the walls with your spider heels hidden in your tennis shoes. From the roof, no one is outside. G.E. only sent a small force against kids. Their arrogance is their undoing. Even in their weakness, no other disciple made it outside except for you. Hopefully, some found a hiding place.

You make it to the woods and take it one tree at a time. There are mines all over the ground. You can't depend entirely on your map. There use to be another disciple's house right after these woods. G.E. would probably search there next if not already. Stick with the plan. Trust no one but your family.

Stay off the roads. The yards near here are not fenced. Keep walking through the backyards and run if you have to. That time is now as a tailless black dog with a cut comes barking and chasing after you. Go! Go! Go!

"Hey!" You almost run into an older lady hanging up her clothes. The basket falls over and the dog runs into a sheet, later colliding into the clothesline pole. The woman runs inside. You have to hurry up!

There is a bicycle left in someone's yard. "No!" You must avoid stealing! You are a disciple! There is always a more excellent way! Time is about to run out!

Eventually, you see an old broken down pick-up truck in someone's backyard. "Get under there now!" Just in time too. The G.E. force that invaded the middle school is going down the street satisfied with their recent spoils. You are just a kid. You could not have made it this far.

You may not make it much further if that snake slithering underneath the truck gets you. "Don't move!" The green snake slithers all around you and finally loses interest in you. The next thirty minutes feels like a day's shift as you pray and think about your next move.

It starts to rain. You definitely have a chance now. You will not be the only one running in the rain. You keep running and don't look back. You are homeward bound. Unfortunately, G.E. is already there. When it rains, it pours.

The good news is that no one's home. Hopefully, word reached them that your school was invaded. You got to get to the meeting place. The farm is not far. You will miss the church services in the barn. Who will be missed more? You or your family, if one of you don't make it there?

The rain picks up as you jet to the farm. Further turbulence is ahead. The corn fields you must crawl through take on a life of their own with the quickening winds. They make way to the rolling thunder stampede coming your way. Your heart beat still outpaces the stampede.

You almost nose dive into the muddy pool of a field from the flying debris and slapping corn fields. The emerging worms and cockroaches will not feast on you yet. No doubt about it. This is just disgusting. You got to accelerate.

The flashing light provides glimpses of death. Then there is darkness. Roll! The lightening on your trail just missed you. Not everything around you was as fortunate.

It's time to get up and take your chances. Death is haunting your either way. The frowning scarecrow tries to take you with him as he falls. Not today! Crashing into the barn doors still hurts, but you are able to walk away.

The doors into darkness have been opened. Something from the shadow emerges, wrapping its arm around your neck. "Freeze disciple! You won't get away this time!"

You feel an object pointed at your skull as the stranglehold tightens. You fall forward to the ground attempting to trip the stranger to the ground. He actually falls on top of you. Before you make another move, the lightning flashes a comforting revelation before you.

"Harvey, what are you doing?" you shouted. "What is your problem?"

"That is not your problem," Harvey said. He's right. "Argh!" "Jerry, just how many times are you going to get ants in your pants?"

"More times than you will beat me at spiderball!" you responded. "Don't rub it in if you want this!" Harvey said. "Okay! Okay!" Those blasted ants!

Harvey throws you a backpack. "You actually made it to the house?" you said. "Of course," Harvey said. Of course, the high school is right near the house. The change of clothes is a lifesaver! "Jerry, you're a mess!" Harvey said.

Later, you ask Harvey how he heard about the siege at the middle school. "Old man Grizzy told me as he was listening to something in the janitor's office," Harvey responded. "I guess you never know who is a disciple," you said. "Never count anyone out." "You're getting worried about the others?" you asked.

"Yeah," Harvey sighed. The waiting game is never easy. It's downright suspenseful.

As the downpour declines, other survivors trickle in. Still, you don't see them. The growing number of candles and lanterns provide flickering glimpses of hope as you wait. "Hope that is seen is not hope: for what a man seeth, why doth he yet hope for? But if we hope for that we see not, then do we with patience wait for it." (From Romans 8:24-25, King James Version) The hope part you keep, but patience continues to dim. Where are they?

Weeping mothers are embraced learning of their children's demise. Tearful fathers latch onto their families with all their might. There is no guaranty they will see each other again pass today. This congregation knows that the local assembly will forever change after today's siege. Some have already departed; others never to return. There are the stubborn still determined to stay no matter what. The challenges of the future have already overshadowed the trials of the past. It is the triumphs that come at the end keeping hope alive. All present, make the most of their moment. Still, they are not here. What moment will you and Harvey have?

Farmer Bill calls the assembly together for prayer. Usually, those who don't make it in by the conclusion of the prayer either did not make it or already moved on. They would not move on without you and Harvey. Still, where are they? The prayer starts with Farmer Bill leading the prayer.

"Heavenly Father in Jesus name we thank you for life and the promise of life more abundantly you have given us. Please Lord, comfort those who lost loved ones this day. Spare those whose fates remain uncertain so that they can complete the work you ordained for them to do. Bless us to keep our joy in the midst of it all because you are with us. Your love for us is greater than any hatred working against us.

Bless us to love others as you have loved us, never hating anyone. Deliver us from evil. Bring our loved ones home. We claim more survivors and victors. Lead us what to do as we rejoice in your name Jesus. Amen."

A rushing wind came through knocking the barn doors open. "People, a G.E. patrol is on their way here!" a familiar voice said.

"Dad!" you and Harvey blurted out. "Where's Cess?" you asked.

"Cecilia is already in the van. We have to go!" Dad said. "Harvey, you don't have to go. We can all hide in the chamber underneath till things cool off," Farmer Bill said to Dad. Dad's mind was made up. Everyone else was going to the underground chamber under the barn. We followed Dad to the van near the side of the barn. "Boys, this place has been compromised. May God help those who remain," Dad said. "Keep quiet and get down on the floor with Cecilia when you get in. People are still thinking I am making pizza deliveries in this van."

"Jerry!" Cecilia whispered from the depths of her gentle heart. You smiled and held your tearful sister's hand. "Cess, it is going to be alright," you said. "We are going to another sanctuary."

"Cess, it's good to see you too," Harvey said. "Oh, hi Harvey," Cess responded. "You're still upset about the salt squares in your tea this morning?" Harvey said. "I hope you get stuck with a spinach pizza!" Cecilia said. "Keep it down back there!" Dad said. Some things never change. Those are the things that keep us going sometimes.

No one said another word as we left town. You will miss Glotown, but Glotown will not miss you. Now that they know who you are, they will want to kill you. Here we go again is spoken again on the facial expressions of you and your siblings as you make eye contact.

Our prayers were answered. A thick fog emerged from the heavens. Many could not see, but we could. We could see that the van barely crossed the bridge before its scheduled opening. We believe the fog helped provide cover for Farmer Bill and other disciples. We do not believe in just the mundane. We have come to expect the supernatural. We live by miracles from a miracle. Many more are needed. Just believe.

Chapter 2: Temporary Sanctuary

We eventually got off the parkway and made a turn into the woods. This is not too far from a park you went to on a field trip. It is hard to believe that you were living in the same place for about four years. It is even harder to believe that a sanctuary may be near here. Still, if Dad drove any further, you would hit one of the cities where word has likely gotten out by now.

"Jerry, you took a risk getting up when you did," Dad said. "We're far along enough now where everybody can get up." Does Dad ever loosen up anymore?

"We might as well," Cecilia said. "Harvey keeps snoring." His snores are right at home with the crickets and frogs who welcome us. We keep going deeper and deeper into the silencing darkness.

The silence was short lived. Harvey's grumbling stomach finally wakes him up. "It must be pizza time," Harvey said. Harvey may be the thinnest of us, but he definitely eats the most. You will miss this van. It even has a power supply for the microwave. Cecilia makes sure to hook everyone up. Dad keeps driving while he eats. No one can blame him. Not even G.E. comes out in this kind of woods unless they have a big tip off. Hopefully, no one tipped them off to where we're going.

"Jerry, just how did you escape from G.E. when they came into the school?" Cecilia asked. "What did you do, Jerry, challenge them to a game of spiderball?" Harvey said. "Harvey, this is serious," Cecilia said. "Go ahead son," Dad said. "Basically, it was the bulb ball and spiderball shoes that saved me, along with Mr. Winsom's sacrifice," you said. "Mr. Winsom was a disciple?" Harvey said. "He was according to G.E. He left the window open for my escape."

"Was Mr. Winsom shot?" Dad asked. "I don't know what happened to him," you said. "G.E. carried him off and I just heard him screaming down the hallway."

"They will make an example out of him," Dad said. "They have a nerve to call themselves men shooting and beating up a bunch of seventh and eighth graders. Did you see anyone else make it out?" "I saw a few other survivors at the barn prayer meeting," you said. "You followed the instructed path?" Dad asked. "All the way," you said. "Good job Jerry," Dad said. "I am proud of you and so glad you're here."

"Yeah, how else can I get my spiderball rematch," Harvey said. "Do you only think of yourself, Harvey?" Cecilia said. "Jerry, are you hurt at all?" "I'm fine, Cess." "You were not fine with that mud suit you had on. You know I bailed you out."

"Harvey, did you go back to the house after you heard about what happened to Jerry's school?" Dad asked. "Umm..." Harvey said. "Harvey, you could have gotten yourself killed or arrested! You always go to the meeting place first. You should know better!"

"Things worked out," Harvey said. "This time," Cecilia said. "Harvey, the change in clothes was a lifesaver for me," you said. "Thanks."

Before you could finish, Harvey opened up the duffel bag he got from the house. He pulled out something that got Cecilia's attention. "Harvey, you saved my favorite doll!" Cecilia said. She grabbed both Harvey and the doll. "I don't want to lose either one of you," Cecilia said. "Please be careful next time. Thank you, Harvey." Tears started to slowly leak from her fragile eyes. As old and battered as that doll is, this remains one of Cecilia's greatest treasures. Mom gave it to her. Cecilia tries so hard to be like her. She always frustrates herself with the same impossible task. We all miss Mom, especially Dad. "Harvey, I love you son," Dad said. Harvey's smile was priceless. "Dad, I…" Harvey said. Dad put on brakes hard.

We just missed the deer that came out of nowhere. You soon hear footsteps on top of the van. A wolf leaps off to pursue his prey. A confrontation is set for the final act of this drama. The deer puts up a fight, but darkness claims him like all the rest. The enforcer got his fresh meat. It is best for you to keep on going.

The lights go out and we enter a cave. "How can we see anything?" Cecilia said. "You don't have to," Dad said. "Just have faith." The van started to sink as you capsized into the underworld. The humming sound of a hidden elevator beneath escorts you further down your destiny. Hopefully, your journey will not end here. There's still nothing you can see. Moments like these definitely inspire you to walk the straight and narrow.

Just as you hit rock bottom, part of the wall revolves and spins everyone to the other side. Then, there is this blinding light promising judgment. "Retina scan complete," said an inhuman voice. "The Redmons are part of the Disciples Network. You may enter the sanctuary." We're home free, at least until a week. That is when a sanctuary council kicks us out to make room for others.

Everyone is now in a dimly lit parking garage. There are enough vehicles here to start a used car lot and maybe even a junk shop. Two men with red vests and laser guns come out to greet you. "Welcome to Sanctuary 56," one of the red vested men said. "Does anyone need emergency care?"

"The Lord kept us once again," Dad said. "Everyone is well." The red vested men embraced us as we got out of the van, happy that more brothers and sisters are still in the land of the living. "Brother Redmon, we can fix up your van while you are here," the other red vested man said. "What can we get if we traded it in for cash?" Dad asked. "Brother Redmon, you will probably need to go to the Visitor Center to get more of the answers you are seeking." For Dad to not even consider modifying the van, where exactly are we going next?

We did not see any familiar faces at the Visitor Center. When we started looking at the directory map, we lost focused on Dad's goal. "Spiderball!" shouted both you and Harvey. "What about The Exchange?" Dad asked. "Dad, I will go with you and help out. Please let Jerry and Harvey play. Jerry's been through so much lately," Cecilia said. "Okay, but just one session, and then meet back here." "Thank you, Dad!"

Spiderball is actually a simple game. Eight balls are launched at you the same time by the server and you need to hit back as many balls with your left and right-hand paddles as you can towards your opponent's court. The balls either one of you miss are caught by moving web score nets and then served again. The game keeps on going until time runs out. Whoever has the highest score wins. The really fun part is wearing shoes and gloves that allow you to stick on walls and ceilings. For safety, every-one has to wear a helmet with a web mask.

"Jerry, are you ready?" Harvey said. "Yes, I'm ready to win," you said. "We'll see about that! I got first serve!" The robo server gets into position and is getting ready to launch eight balls based on the serving combo selected by Harvey. You have to get ready. Instinct must now replace thought. The robo server gives the green light. Go!

Left! Right! Up! Down! Climb! Jump! Right! Left! Missed! Back! Right! Left! Climb! Right! Right! Down! Up! Left! Left!

Missed! Missed! Duck! Right! Right! Spin! Down! Up! Left! Right! Left! Right! Jump! Missed! Up! Left! Back! Climb! Right! Right! Down! Jump! Left! Right! Left! Left! Right! Right! Down! Missed! Right! Duck! Up! Down! Back! Back! Climb! Left! Left! Right! Right! Jump! Left! Right! Missed! Up! Duck! Left! Right! Crisscross! Left! Missed! Jump! Up! Down! Spin! Left! Right! Left! Left! Over! It takes you both a while to get used to the slowdown of reality. "Game," you said. "You got lucky once again," said a disappointed Harvey. "This is all about skill." you said. "Next time, the close call will go my way." Having confidence in another rematch reflects hope to be alive for another day. It is time to get back to Dad and Cecilia.

When you see Dad and Cecilia, you noticed a smile on his face and extra bags in Cecilia's hand. Dad must have gotten a good deal for the van at The Exchange. "We got something for you," Cecilia said. She opened up the bags and Harvey and I saw new spiderball shoes and gloves in our sizes. "Thank you, Dad, and Cess," we said. "You're welcome," they said. "Let's get to our room. We have to get an early start in the morning to pick up more supplies. This is a good sanctuary to stock up." Dad said.

Our room was not much, but it was clean. Carpet was too much of a luxury here. There were two sets of bunk beds with each set having a bunk bed above the other and one light bulb in between both bunk bed sets as the only light in the room other than the bathroom light. The bathroom only had an aging toilet and sink that was at least cleaner than what you will see at some gas stations. The tile on the floor did remind you of a gas station. The room had a neutral smell to it, nothing to make it feel like home or a prison. We miss our old home in Glotown already. You would not be surprised if Dad tries to rush the sanctuary council's decision on our next destination. After we had our family prayer, Harvey and I stayed up later testing out our new spiderball gear. "Do you think we will get assigned to a place like Glotown?" you asked Harvey while both of you climbed the wall near your bunk beds. "I hope not," Harvey said. "I am tired of the country." "You know how Dad hates cities after what happened to Mom," you whispered. "This council may not give us a choice," Harvey said. "Harvey, you may very well get your wish." We went no further with this conversation and turned off the one light in the room. You are nervous about moving back to the city again. The last time we were in a city, Mom was killed. Dad almost killed her murderer. All of us barely escaped being captured. Dad really cut it close and we almost became orphans. Harvey was not ready to lead us then. Who will lead us if that time does come?

With the way Dad has been purchasing supplies and gear the last couple of days, it is almost as if he believes he knows the way to Sanctuary 7. The first six sanctuaries were eventually found by the so called "gods" and their enforcers and most of the disciples in them were killed. Many sanctuaries have sprung up since that time, but Sanctuary 7 is supposed to be the only sanctuary that cannot be found and once you are there, you do not have to leave. You never have to worry about G.E. in this life and the next. One day after breakfast, Harvey goes off to a temporary job within Sanctuary 56 to earn some more money. As soon as Harvey leaves, Dad approaches Cecilia and you.

"There is something I must show you, Jerry and Cecilia," Dad said. "Follow me." We followed Dad to the sanctuary's library. One of the assistants escorted us to the storage area inferring that there was something we needed to pick up. Dad whispered for us to hold his hand

and trust him. We walked in faith right through the wall.

The library outside looked like a yard sale collection placed on the shelves, but the small computer room we just found ourselves in looked like something from a spy network. Everything was 3-D and touchable. Holograms of all types and colors surrounded us, but nothing made a sound. A floating message also circled around us instructing, "DO NOT TALK! PUT ON THE EAR PIECES AND CHEW A PIECE OF GUM!" Afterwards, we could hear again.

A somber, bald headed man with glasses came up to us. "Do not ask questions," the bald-headed man said. "Follow me." We made it to another room and a 3-D holographic head appeared of a man with a beard and dark skin. "This is Philip," Dad said. "He came from Sanctuary 7 and provides carefully guarded clues to its location. The problem is that his clues are scattered and oftentimes encrypted. Even when deciphered, no one knows what he is talking about. It is not known if he ever made it back to Sanctuary 7 or is even alive. Still, pay attention." Dad told us about Philip after Mom died. This particular sanctuary must be the third clue Dad received. He told us about the other two clues He and Mom knew.

The Philip hologram started to speak. "Peace is not based on where you search for, but how you are found. When your heart is revealed, allow what is necessary to lead the way. Death may have to come before life. Your destiny will choose which comes first. Then, you will be in the right place. You must..." Then Philip abruptly faded away leaving behind a puzzled, sometimes frustrated audience. "May it be the Lord's will for you to understand this," the bald-headed man said. "We still have not found the way there yet." "Thank you, my brother," Dad said. "Let's go now kids." Dad did not want us to say a word about this to Harvey. Harvey talks too much. By the time Harvey got back from working, Cecilia and I were already in bed. Harvey mentioned to Dad that he was able to find work the next day as well.

When Harvey came back from work this time, everyone was up in the room. Dad wanted to tell everyone the sanctuary council's decision at the same time. We were all in suspense, even more so, due to Dad not eating all day and being of fewer words. After coming back from the council hearing, Dad had been sweating, praying, and moaning for hours. "Harvey, sit down," Dad said. "Harvey, Jerry, and Cecilia, this sanctuary's council has given us new identities and one-way transportation to live in the city of Allure. May the will of the Lord be done." No one said a word, but no one slept at the same time. Being sent to Allure is like a death sentence for a disciple. Will you even live to see your fourteenth birthday? Mom, you may be seeing me again soon.

Chapter 3: Tagged

Before boarding the ship to Allure, we had to memorize our new identities. Even though in our hearts, we know we will always be a Redmon, for now, we must go by Johnson. You are now George Johnson. Dad goes by Ted Johnson. Harvey got stuck with Thomas Johnson. Cecilia fared better with a name somewhat to her liking, Chloe Johnson. Dad warned us that until our cover is blown, we are to use our new names at all times, both in public and private. Considering where we are going, how long will these names or we ourselves last?

The line to board Allure is always long. "Enter ye in at the strait gate: for wide is the gate, and broad is the way, that leadeth to destruction, and many there be which go in thereat:" (From Matthew 7:13, King James Version) The clouds gather as you progress through the end of the line and start to weep with what becomes heavy downpour. Now, your time comes.

"Bzzt...may I see your ticket and identification?" The floating droid asked. "Here you go," you said. The floating droid scans your ticket and id card. "All cleared. Enjoy your trip." The droid's slow, slurred voice was anything but clear. These cheap droids malfunction in the rain. The Disciples Network timed it perfectly. Hopefully, security at Allure will not uncover your false information. You run on board with the rest of your family. There is definitely something brewing.

Even inside, there is no escape from the storm. The horn sounds off and you sail off to face the winds of change. "We are going to make it there," Dad said. You wish he was equally confident about us surviving Allure. "Thomas, let's go to the mess hall and get some food right now. George and Chloe, stay in the room unless it starts to flood." Dad always plans ahead. He must be expecting this storm to get worse.

"George, do you think we should even unpack?" Chloe asked. "Chloe, this storm is going to be rough and we should only take things out when we must have them," you said. "It's going to be that bad?" "Yeah."

"Je-George, don't you just get tired of this sometimes?" Chloe said. Chloe places her head on your shoulder and you put your arm around her as you both sit on top of one of the small bunk beds. This small cabin does not have a couch or more than one chair. "Chloe, we will get through this like everything else, together," George said. "George, I love yo-oah!"

Already, the ship started to rock from side to side. "Chloe, hang on!" George said. Just then, a suitcase on the top bunk fell down. "That was close, George," Chloe said. The see saw continued and the only warning provided was through an intercom no one understood. The message sent by the roaring thunder was loud and clear, we are in for quite a storm.

"Chloe, let's grab what we can and be ready to head out when Dad returns," George said. "Okay," Chloe responded. We kept going from downhill to uphill as we gathered the few things we brought with us. Then, things went rapidly downhill. The lights went off. The lightning made its presence known, even at this lower level. The screaming overheard outside in the halls and other cabins did not make things better. Here come the looters!

As soon as we heard another woman scream, a rat jumped on Chloe's shoulder. "Eewwww!" Chloe said. You knock the rat off before he can bite Chloe. A loud thumping on the door puts the rat to flight. Chloe, must have alerted the looters! "Let us in!" someone said.

"George!" "Chloe"! That sounds like Dad! Is that Dad down the hall or in front of the door?

You pull a bat out of your backpack and hand Chloe a knife. The door knob turns. Then the door comes open. You swing your bat, but just manage to break a flash light belonging to one of your intruders. Chloe gets back. Then someone grabs the bat from you! Uh-Oh!

"George and Chloe, stop this now!" "Dad!" you and Chloe said. "Don't forget about me," Thomas said, as he slammed the door shut. "It's bad out there," Dad said. Thomas wrapped our sole chair around the door knob through the center hole. "Everyone, let's eat while we can." After we blessed our food and started eating, another loud thumping came at the door. The thumping got louder and louder. We became silent as our heart beats went into full gear. The invasion began.

"Ow!" a stranger said. Chloe had stabbed this man in the leg. Dad's shock glove took care of him and the other looter. Everyone was ready to go with luggage in hand. Then a pipe burst further down the hall released a vapor putting the other looters to flight. "Let's go!" We followed Dad's lead and went the other way.

"Come this way!" a crewman said with his flashlight. We made it to higher ground to see the lightning show. Just in time too, considering how the lower levels started to flood. "Thomas!" you yelled. Lightning just missed him. Everyone made it to the shelter and was given raincoats. In the air, you can see faces, none friendly. The worse is not over.

The storm takes us for quite a ride and we start to sink. Dad said nothing out loud the whole time. He just kept looking up whispering something. Then comes a whirlpool to bring about a grand finale, which none of us may be able to emerge from. Thomas tells everyone that he loves us as we go in circles. Dad says nothing. Chloe cries. Your frustration gets the best of you as you shout, "No!" to the storm.

Then something amazing happens. It literally feels like a large hand emerges from the river and places the ship in the palm of his hand. Everyone hangs on and we are taken through the eye of the storm and literally placed in a calm river. The rest of the trip is quiet, with few spoken words and even fewer questions answered. Allure awaits. Your paths will cross.

Then, that day finally came. "We're here!" Thomas said. For whatever reason, he always wanted to be in a city. He got his wish this time. We all wanted to take a look. We have been sheltered and napping for too long. No one had the best words to describe this place.

The water around the ship became red. The ship had to come to a dead stop as it approached a tall gate with two large statues, one on each side. There was a ship in front of us. The left statue has an eagle's head on a shapely woman's body while the right statue has a lion's head on a muscular man's body. The eagle head statue's eyes started to glow and blue lasers emerged from her eyes scanning the whole ship in front us. The lion head statue pulled out his right arm and then gave a thumb down with his right hand. The eagle head statue's eyes glowed once more, but this time emitting red lasers. These lasers set the ship on fire and piranhas emerged from the red river to devour those who tried to escape her judgment. We were next.

The eagle head statue scanned our ship as well but chirped something we did not understand. Then, the lion head status pulled out his right arm once again. This time, he gave a thumb up. The gate doors start to open and a light emerges to overshadow the darkness.

We hear a type of music throughout the atmosphere that is soothing yet requiring reverence. The waters here are dyed purple. We pass through statues of various sizes and degree of importance, shown through the gold, silver, and bronze selectively used. This was once the home of the man-made gods and their stench still remains here. A false hope is the only death sentence that people willingly enter. The hypocrisies of the haves and have nots are still marooned here. Justice is only as good as what you have to offer.

Allure is a metropolis with an expanding hunger for souls. Its numerous skyscrapers will put even the plans for the Tower of Babel to shame. There are numerous coliseums to appease the bloodthirsty, enough museums to poison the minds of the blinded intellectuals, an abundance of shops, restaurants, and casinos to make the rich poor, overbearing clubs and bars forever breeding new generations of alcoholics and short-lived entertainers, and unlimited venues to entice a lustful imagination. The population grows to keep up with Allure's deadly appetite.

In spite of the pageantry and the hype associated with it, Allure still shows the appearance of a fading beauty whose glory has departed. The man-made gods left for the moon and left this city as a memorial dedicated to their arrogance. A memorial is for recognition, not for true growth and lasting evolution. When the fantasy fades away, the lusts fail to provide the same level of satisfaction, and pride is humbled by something, someone greater, Allure will then have nothing left to offer.

The horn sounds off once again and we set anchor. No one is reluctant to leave the ship behind because of the intensity of the journey. The destination you have arrived to will present an even greater challenge. The stakes are higher and the temptations are greater.

G.E. officers are all over the place at the welcome center. You and the rest of the family are directed to one of the citizenship lines. An escalator takes you to a lower level. An unusually tall G.E. officer is behind you as you proceed through the double doors. The citizenship process is completely automated now. Still, you will now learn how prepared you are for this moment.

You are praying that the special eye drops everyone took at Sanctuary 56 have not worn off and will get you pass the retina scan. Check! Success! Ow! A needle pricked your finger to make sure that your blood does not match the blood of any of the felons or disciples stored within the database. It is Dad who most concerns you, but he passes this test too. Of course, there is the irritating urine sample that is nothing more than a nuisance. Everyone's papers and id cards are scanned and thankfully checked out okay with the system. We are then forced to say, "The gods are with Allure and I am proud to become a citizen of Allure." We are then granted conditional citizenship to Allure and a G.E. officer tells you which subway train to go on. That same tall G.E. officer who walked behind you earlier now whispers something to the G.E. officer who pointed you to the right train. As you and your family walk closer to the direction of the train stop, that same tall G.E. officer continues to walk in your direction.

You and your family get on the train and you notice the same G.E. officer riding the train car directly behind, separated by a transparent emergency door. You want to say something to Dad or Thomas, but do not want to seem obvious either. This G.E. officer does not get off the train until you get off.

As you walk through your new neighborhood, which is a typical urban jungle failing to be as tamed as its distant uptown neighbors, you see the same G.E. officer walking from behind when you turn your head. You turn your head again and he is gone. Has your cover been blown already? Was the citizenship process too good to be true? Will you be arrested before you even see your new home? Have you been tagged?

Another problem emerges as soon as you reach your new home, which appears to be a high-rise apartment. There are numerous men and women hanging out, smoking and drinking outside near the apartment entrance. When they see you, they stop what they are doing. Before they, Dad, or anyone else makes a move, the mysterious G.E. officer reappears. "They are with me," the G.E. officer said. "If you or anyone else in this place ever harms or harasses this family, I will personally come back and purge whoever is responsible. Spread the word. Do you understand me?" Everyone outside nodded their heads.

Then, the G.E. officer looked in your direction. "Come follow me. I want to talk with you," the G.E. officer said. He led everyone to the basement area of the apartment. This is definitely a discrete location to shock someone. Usually, G.E. officers like to shock and arrest people in front of as large of an audience as possible.

"What do you want with us?" Dad asked. "Lower your voice," the G.E. officer said. "Let's not make it hard."

Dad said nothing else. For a short period of time, the two men just stared each other down. "Don't try to reach for anything in your pocket," the G.E. officer said. Dad paused. "Let's go inside this room." The G.E. officer had a device which unlocked the door without a key.

"We can talk now," the G.E. officer said. "For whatever reason, the monitoring equipment does not work well for basement areas in the buildings around here." Dad still said nothing.

"For the short time we have to talk, you must realize that I am on your side citizen. With the overflow in this apartment building, you were given one of the few apartments in the basement area. Where we are is your new home," the G.E. officer said. "How do you know this?" Dad asked. "I am a disciple too."

We were shocked. "I am Officer Albatross," Albatross said. "I see," Dad said. "I am your Disciple Network contact while you are in Allure. You can only talk freely in the basement areas of the old buildings. For everywhere else, you are closely monitored. Only pray silently in a resting position. For now, trust no one else here other than me. Within a month, I will introduce you to one of the disciple fellowship congregations, but still trust no one else for the next several months until I tell you otherwise. Don't forget to take "The Tour" soon or else they will become suspicious of you. Here is my pager number, but don't call me unless there is emergency. We will be in touch." Dad extends his hand and says, "Thank you Brother."

Chapter 4: New Day

We left in pairs in the morning. Chloe went with Dad and you left with Thomas. As you and Thomas get on the train, you noticed how lifeless everyone is in what is supposed to be a lively place. The daily grinds of life can take away from even the best and bring out the worst. As soon as everyone is seated, the train takes off like a rollercoaster. You have to admit, "You like this!"

The brakes that send you back to reality finally intersect with your stop. As you and Thomas get off the train and head up the escalator, you notice propaganda on the manmade gods all over the place. You don't get to read most of the propaganda due to having to concentrate on keeping up with Thomas throughout this heavy crowd. At least as soon as you leave the train station, you see your new school, Mary B. Ellis Middle School.

"All right George, give the guys a laugh and the girls your number," Thomas said. "Don't get played this time Thomas," you said. "I have learned this time. See ya". "Bye Thomas." A new day awaits.

"WELCOME TO GODHOOD," is the first message that you see from the banner hanging up as you enter the school doors. As a part of your welcome, you walk through a metal detector and your school id is scanned for entry. "Cleared," the God's Enforcer officer said. This school is full of God's Enforcer officers. In spite of their presence, a fight between two guys breaks out. Two God's Enforcer officers quickly come and slam both guys into the lockers. "Send them to Rehab," one of the God's Enforcer officers said. "Everyone get to your classes!"

As you rush to class, you accidentally bump into someone. "Excuse me, I am sorry," you said. "That is okay," She said. When you make eye contact, you notice a beauty unfamiliar to you. Her skin is dark and rich as someone from the African motherland. Her short black hair uncovers a hidden curiosity that quickly dominates your thoughts. Her clear nails display a perceived chastity. Her voice beckons you like a siren. "I'm George." She does not respond and keeps on going.

You make it into a crowded classroom which feels more like an auditorium. As you make your way down, it initially appears that everyone is too busy talking with their own clique to notice you. Then, a paper ball hits your head. As you turn around to find who threw the paper ball at you, you fail to notice the small laser ball used for school devices on the next step and it trips you just enough to fall. Well, Thomas is right. You did give the guys a laugh and as a bonus, the girls too. No one will probably want to give you their number though.

The chorus of laughter is broken up by the dimming of lights as you take a seat. This must be when the teacher comes in. The teacher suddenly appears, but not in a way that you expect.

"Greetings class," a three-dimensional hologram of an older man said. "Welcome George Johnson." You pause. "Are you okay from your fall?" the holographic teacher asked. "Yes," you said. "Let it be known that we are watching you and the gods see you all. Who among you will make history or be history? Let us continue on with our history lecture."

This history class is nothing like the ones you have experienced before. The rural towns you came from always taught the history of how things were before the birth of the gods. Right in the lesson's introduction, the class is told to disregard the B.C. and A.D. timelines. The harsh words spoken were, "Jesus Christ is dead and He is not coming back for His deluded followers that remain attached to such a fantasy. This is why we have the gods, to bring reality to divinity and hope. We no longer have to hope for better days, we can make new millenniums ourselves. While you are in Allure, you shall focus on the A.G. timeline, the arrival of the gods. Nothing else really matters before then." You have to put up with this propaganda for a full ninety minutes. This lesson primarily focused on some of the history of Allure, the good old days before the gods abandoned it like a politician drops a harlot when morning arrives. Allure has definitely seen better times. Her present state is a father's worst nightmare of his daughter.

At least the math class is smaller. Unfortunately, there is no real teacher. The holographic image is multiple pre-recordings of people partnered with artificial intelligence. Everyone follows along on interactive tablets. The computer instructor follows your personal progress on the tablet and the screen points out learning tips tailored for you. Math ends with the computer instructor telling everyone, "Those who do not know math and science are prisoners of imagination instead of being gods in reality," You then must click that you completed the lesson and sign off. "You can only have faith in what you know." Those final words are truer than it thinks. You know the truth and it shall make you free.

Finally, lunchtime is here. Dad always has you buy lunch because he usually just does not have the time to pack everyone a lunch. You really miss mom's lunches and her even more so. At least buying lunch will decrease the amount of time you will have to seat around the cafeteria. The food is far from alluring. The mystery meat accompanied by raw seasoned vegetables and dry fruit will have to do. Now comes the hard part.

As you make your way to the tables, some frown while others turn their heads. The seats quickly fill up when you are around and additional people are quick to shake their heads and tell you empty seats are reserved for people, who you suspect will likely never come. You finally see a table with empty chairs ahead of you with only two people at the table. One of the faces is actually familiar, the girl of your dreams that you encountered earlier is there! You quickly make your way over there, ignoring the strange person who is also sitting there.

As soon as you get to the table, she leaves without saying anything to you. You are left sitting near a guy with a robot suit on. "Who are you?" the guy in the robot suit said. "George," you said. He then says nothing. Who is this guy? "You have my name. What's yours?"

"Trevor," the guy in the robot suit said. "It is good to meet you Trevor," you said. "George, have you been on the tour yet?" "No."

"When I went on the tour, the werewolves did this to me and I have to wear this monkey suit just to keep breathing," Trevor said. "Werewolves?" you said. "If you don't want to believe me, you better believe this, stay away from Kim!" "Kim, who?" you replied.

"I know you want Kim Guardia, but she's mine," Trevor said. "I do not see a ring on her finger or yours," you said. "Do not try me George." You walk away before this gets nastier than the food you have leftover.

You are so upset that you fail to notice the milk carton on the floor and trip over it as your tray flies sideways slamming into Trevor's face. He throws some of your old leftovers back at your face and shouts something about your mother. Both of you got everyone's attention in the cafeteria. The fight is on! How do you fight a guy in a robot suit?

For emergency escapes, Dad did give you a set of little dissolving plastic balls with a sensor in it that will trigger most ceiling fire extinguishers. You reach into your pocket to seemingly pull out a mechanical pencil but activate the sensor. Before Trevor can punch you, all of the cafeteria fire extinguishers go off showering everyone with water and foam. As people take flight, the fight is interrupted. As you reach the door, a God's Enforcer officer is there to greet you. "Get down on your knees now," the God's Enforcer officer said. You comply to not get shocked. "You are coming to Rehab with me now!" As you walk, you notice Trevor being carried away and a long wire from his back exposed with foam. You hear whispers of him being trampled and you are in trouble.

You are escorted to a quiet hallway leading down to a dimly lit staircase taking you to a basement area. A metal door opens and your ears are opened to the horrors others are experiencing. Before you can respond, a blindfold is placed around your eyes and you are thrown down a chute where you feel a heater drying you off as you slide down into a couch. You also felt several robotic hands inspecting you and scanning you along the way. Your blindfold is also removed.

A pale skinned man with a bald head is there waiting for you. "George, you are new here," the pale skinned man said. "Yes," you said. "Let me educate you quickly, young man. We have the highest of standards in Allure and you are going to use your free period to think about them. Do not worry. You will make your biology class on time. This amoeba droid will get you up to speed quickly"

This disgusting tiny liquid robot is forced into your left nostril and you black out, awakening to another world going in hyper speed. You see several teenagers turning into werewolves and shot down while hearing a voice saying, "You become a monster when you reject the gods and the gods will kill you." Then, some magicians appear and they are stepped on like insects by a god's big foot while hearing a voice saying, "There is no power greater than the gods. Obey! Obey!" You then see several men and women transform from weak, depressed people to super beings full of joy and strength while hearing a voice saying, "If you obey, you will be rewarded with longer mortality or even immortality itself. Obey! Obey!" The same messages keep repeating themselves with different images becoming more surreal and fast forwarding at different speeds. You head feels like it is exploding as the amoeba droid dissolves. You are left a screaming mess and then wake up right at the entrance of your biology class.

Various people stare at you but say nothing to you. You are too spaced out to notice that Kim Guardia is sitting right behind you, leaving a note on your desk. This is the first class where you see a teacher in person. The whole class is a slide show featuring clips on how various animals were transformed when the god experiments were conducted on them before humans. You will be dissecting clones of some of the mutated animals throughout the year. Is this teacher really human? All of this is intended to show you the greatness of the manmade gods.

This school day is over and Thomas is leaning over right of the school entrance barely able to stand. "Ready, George?" Thomas asked. "Yes, but are you okay Thomas?" "Food poisoning from the mystery meat." Thomas said. You help Thomas get to the train, praying that he will not throw up along the way. Your headache keeps you distracted. This is one of those days.

As soon as you get home, Thomas runs into the bathroom and vomits out a big one, followed by a series of diarrhea. Count your blessings that this apartment does have a second half bathroom. Then you collapse.

You wake up and you see Dad, Chloe, and Thomas. "George, what happened?" Dad asked. You give him a recap of everything that happened except using one of the plastic sensor balls and what happened during free period. Unfortunately, you do not even remember what happened during free period. Of course, Dad admonishes you to not continue fighting and avoiding trouble at all costs. He also tells you, "Emergency protocols are not to be used for personal fights," Dad said. "Sorry, Dad," you said. He knew that you used a plastic ball. "George, I am just happy that you okay. I do not want you to end up at Sister Southern's Hospital where I work at. It is not somewhere you want to be, even if you work there." Dad does not like his new job. "George, I made friends with several girls today at school who love wearing dresses like me," Chloe said. "Chloe, I am glad that your first day turned out better than mine," you said. "George, do you think they are disciples?" "Remember, where we are Chloe." Chloe smiles in response.

Thomas does not bother to talk about his school day, but you later hear him talking to someone over the phone in the bedroom with the door closed. This reminds you about a note you got from Kim Guardia you somehow forgot about. What really happened at school? You open the note and it reads, "Thank you. Give me your number. We will talk later." This is truly a new day with new opportunities. You sleep well with your thoughts being refocused.

Also Available from Apostolic
Pentecostal Alliance Books LLC

www.apabooksllc.com

Using the Power Within

Learn how to obtain and use the supernatural power God ordained for you to have to change your life and fulfill your true destiny. Available in printed and e-book editions.

Happiness as an Independent Variable Second Edition

Wouldn't you rather be happy instead of sad, angry, or worried? Our traditional perceptions and common understandings of happiness oftentimes fail to lead us to true happiness. With this book, you will discover that happiness must be treated as an independent variable if you are to have and maintain the long-term state of happiness. This is available in printed and e-book editions.

www.ingramcontent.com/pod-product-compliance
Lightning Source LLC
Chambersburg PA
CBHW071013120726
47910CB00004B/1503